This Book
presented to the

CHURCH
LIBRARY
by

RAEDELLE & HARRY BROOKS

August 1993

Code 4386-21, No. 1, Broadman Supplies, Nashville, Tenn. Printed in USA

ITSY-BITSIES Storybooks™
Woolly
Has Two Dozen Sisters!

Written by Gary Poole
Illustrated by Kathleen Smith-Fitzpatrick

MODERN PUBLISHING
A Division of Unisystems, Inc.
New York, New York 10022

Woolly Lamb was an only son.
His parents had just that one!

But they did have a bunch of girls
And each one had a bunch of curls.

Each one wore a frilly bow,
And knew how to play the piccolo.

They liked dolls, and "house" and tea,
But you never saw one climb a tree.

Which is what Woolly liked to do...

And play catch and wrestle, too.

So he set off to find some boys
Who liked his favorite games and toys.

He came upon a lively clan
Of brothers playing Kick-the-Can.

Woolly had a splendid day,
Playing all the games he liked to play.

He asked them: "May I be your brother?"
"Of course!" they agreed amongst each other.

Then, much to Woolly Lamb's surprise,
The boys pulled off their caps and ties,
Which they'd used as their disguise.

They tied up ribbons in their curls.
Woolly cried: "My stars! You're girls!"

"We're your sisters and we made believe
We were boys so you wouldn't leave.

There's no need to run away.
We love to play the games you play!"

Now in between "house" and dolls, and teas

Woolly and his sisters are climbing trees!